OCEANIC HEARTS

Mansi Aggarwal

Published By

Redgrab Books Pvt. Ltd.

942, Mutthiganj, Prayagraj, 211003

www.redgrabbooks.com

contact@redgrabbooks.com

Price in india : 200/- INR

First published by Redgrab Books in 2023

Printed and bound in India

Cover Design & Typesetting by Redgrab Books team

ISBN : 978-93-95697-37-8

"To see a world in a grain of sand
and heaven in a wild flower
Hold infinity in the palms of your hand
and eternity in an hour."
William Blake

Contents

Part 4

ACKNOWLEDGEMENT

I declare my love and admiration for my husband Arindam Bhattacharjee without whom this book would not have been possible. I am filled with adoration for the advice and affection of my sister Nancy Agarwal.

I also thank my family and friends whose love and support kept me going.

PART 1

CHAPTER 1

"Memories! They keep the person alive long after they are gone," thought Anusha while in a cab, on her way to the airport. It was six o'clock in the morning. The sun was barely out and the Christmas lights were still tinkling. Anusha snuggled her hands in the pockets of her overcoat and looked outside pensively. The crows were drinking water from a puddle on the road and the cab entered a boulevard. It had rained the previous night and the damp earth brought a whiff of isolation to Anusha. The fog which took over after the rains, reminded her of the cold stinging spite of loneliness. She closed her eyes and in the recesses of her mind felt a familiar warmth. A warmth which had always protected her. The cab, now running on the highway, took an exit reaching the Indira Gandhi International Airport of Delhi.

The airport was quite full of activity even in the wee hours of the morning. It was the holiday season and people were rushing to meet their loved ones. The flights were getting delayed due to the fog and the airport was a sight of chaos. Anusha checked in her luggage and grabbed the only vacant and a bit solitary chair at the end of Gate 7. Her flight to Bangalore had got delayed by an hour. She tugged her handbag and slept for a while when the announcement woke her up. There was a further delay. Anusha felt a slight stiffness in her throat. She moved towards the food courts. A dreary feeling engulfed her. She ordered a filter coffee from her favourite South Indian eatery hoping to find some respite from the cold. Sipping on it she looked around to find a seat and spotted an available chair opposite the table occupied by a man in his late twenties, around her age, eating a sandwich and might be listening to the music with his earphones on. She gestured at him to ask if she might occupy that chair, and he pulled the table towards himself to make room for her. Anusha looked at him. He was wearing thick nerdy glasses, was clean-shaven and had long slender fingers with which he was holding his sandwich. He was not handsome but there was a certain serenity to his face which made Anusha comfortable sharing a table with him. They both were immersed in their worlds when a kid running towards the adjacent table shook theirs. Anusha spilt her coffee on the table.

"I am so sorry," said Anusha, wiping the coffee with the tissues in her hand.

The man removed his earphones and looked at Anusha with his big round eyes which he had widened in his curiosity.

"It is ok. It's not your fault."

"That kid!" They both spoke simultaneously and cleaned the table together.

"What music are you listening to?"

"Sorry!"

Anusha asked again, mustering a little courage which was generally required while talking to a stranger.

"What music are you listening to?"

The man chuckled, "Oh! It's not music. It's an audiobook by Murakami."

“Murakami! He is one of my favourite writers. Which one are you listening to?"

“Sputnik Sweetheart”

“It is hypnotic. I loved the character of Miu.”

"Oh, I have not reached that point."

“I am sorry. But don’t worry I have not revealed much.”

The man smiled.

“Anusha” Anusha extended her hand.

“Aman” He replied taking her hand gently. “Where are you heading?” He continued.

“Bangalore. Came here for a training programme. And you?”

“Was here for a conference, going back home now, Pune.”

“Pune is a pleasant city. The food is not that great but I enjoy the youthful vibe of the place. One of my cousins stays there.”

“I have never been to Bangalore. Hope to visit it someday.”

Anusha was not listening to Aman anymore. Her mind had wandered towards a couple who had sat next to them. They seemed to be newly married. The wife was wearing the traditional red bangles which a Punjabi Indian bride usually wears during her wedding, and vows to wear them for a few weeks and sometimes even a year, after the marriage. It covered most of her forearms as the tradition required. They were laughing and chatting and the husband was looking at her full of love and affection.

Suddenly something triggered and Anusha became numb. Her hand started trembling and she tightened her fist to control it.

Flashes of the past disturbed her. She started to sweat and shut her eyes. Aman noticed this. He shook her hand and tried to undermine the trigger. Anusha was still struggling with her sudden anxiety attack. Aman rushed to get her water and Anusha gulped it down. Tears rolled down her eyes.

"Hey! Hey! It's all right. Nothing has happened. Look at me."

Anusha still kept her eyes closed.

"Take deep breaths. I'm here. Calm down."

Anusha opened her eyes and excused herself to use the washroom. She splashed her face with water, took out a sachet of pills from her bag and swallowed one. She looked at herself in the mirror, rearranged her hair and tried to get her composure back. Aman waited for her to return. An announcement was made. It was a call for boarding for Anusha's flight. Aman heard the announcement and felt uneasy as if something he had valued was leaving him. Anusha was walking towards the cafeteria when she heard the announcement. She saw Aman shifting in his chair on hearing it. She was embarrassed and still perturbed by the whole incident.

"How are you feeling now?

"Better! Thank You!" "It was nice meeting you."

"It was nice meeting you too."

"Thank you for your help."

Anusha turned away and paced towards the boarding gate. Aman sat there looking at her for a long time till she disappeared down the elevator.

CHAPTER 2

It was a gorgeous day. Anusha was getting engaged to her long-time boyfriend Karan. They had been together since their management college days. Karan had first seen Anusha at the fresher's party. Anusha was a trained Bharatnatyam dancer and she had performed on stage that day. Karan had fallen in love at first sight. It took him several weeks to finally get to talk to her. She was sitting in the library alone, wearing black framed glasses and strands of her wavy hair were falling on her face which she was pushing at the back of her ears with her fingers. Her ears were small and she had an angelic face of a cherub. Karan walked up to her and took the seat next to her.

"Hi."

"Hi," Anusha replied to his pleasantry as if asking a question.

"I saw your dance that day. You were terrific."

"Thanks"

"We are in the same class." "Karan"

Anusha shook his hand.

"And no need to tell yours, I know it's Anusha."

Anusha smiled and Karan became the happiest man in the world.

From the next day, Karan and Anusha were inseparable. They

were together in class, in the canteen, in the library and even after college. They became the love birds of the college. Everyone knew about them and vouched for their love story. They remained like that for the next two years till their placements. Anusha joined a private bank and a financial consultancy hired Karan.

When Karan proposed Anusha for marriage it was not a surprise for anyone. Even their families knew and were waiting for them to tie the knot.

The engagement day was well planned. Family, friends and guests were all present and Karan was waiting for Anusha to come and join him. Anusha, entered the hall looking ethereal in a bright golden Banarasi saree, as any would-be bride would have looked, a bride full of love. Karan looked at her dewy-eyed. That day she was the most beautiful woman on earth for him. Anusha saw Karan all emotional and winked at him making him blush. Rings were exchanged and everyone cheered.

It was Saturday and a few weeks before marriage. Anusha and Karan were returning from a late-night dinner with Karan driving the car. The music volume was up. A romantic oldie was playing and they both were singing along. Karan while singing looked at Anusha. The next moment, a puppy suddenly came in front of the car. Karan pulled the brakes to save the puppy. The car screeched and crossed over the divider and fell upside down on the other side of the road. Anusha somehow managed to crawl out of the car. Blood was oozing out of her forehead. She came running towards Karan. He was unconscious. Panicked, Anusha called for the ambulance. The sound of ambulance yelped through the dead silence of the night.

Karan and Anusha were rushed to the hospital. Anusha gained consciousness the next day. With her parents by her side, she was told that Karan had succumbed to his injuries. Anusha's whole world fell apart in that instance. She became numb as if frozen in time.

CHAPTER 3

Anusha came home weary and exhausted. She opened the door with her keys. Everyone in the house was already asleep. She went into her room, kept her luggage on the side and looked at the candid picture of Karan and herself laughing away with their arms intertwined with each other. They looked happy. A smile spread across Anusha's face. She opened the "Karan" folder on her mobile and started browsing all the photos of Karan. She never realised when she slept away with the phone in her hand.

Akriti, Anusha's younger sister entered her room in the morning. The room was dark and had a dank vibe to it. Akriti pulled the curtains and a fresh ray of sunlight lit up the room. Anusha opened her eyes and squinted them, unwilling to wake up. Her phone was lying on the bed with the "Karan" folder still open. Akriti saw that and became concerned about her sister. She woke Anusha up and almost lift her off the bed. Anusha looked fatigued and pale. Her eyes were red. Akriti braved a smile on her face and greeted Anusha.

"Good morning Sha!" "How was your trip."

"It was fine."

"Come, take a shower and get ready." "We are waiting outside for you at breakfast," saying that Akriti left the room.

All four of them were now at the dining table, Anusha, Akriti and their parents. Akriti was dressed up in her lawyer attire. She was two years younger than Anusha, and though she was the youngest, she held the family together with her patience and pragmatism. She loved Anusha unconditionally and after Karan had gone she was Anusha's only confidante. Anusha's father, Pradip, was reading the newspaper and was chomping on the aloo parathas Anusha's mother had made. Anusha's mother Seema was a homemaker. Seema had devoted all her life to making that house a home. She had sacrificed her flourishing job to take care of the home and her two daughters. Both Seema and Pradip had raised their daughters to be independent. But after Karan's death, the house was no longer the same. Anusha could not get over the incident and move ahead. She was slipping away and her family was seeing that every day helplessly.

"We are thinking of going to Ooty for a few days. It would be a nice family vacation". "Both of you, apply for a leave from your office", said Anusha's father gingerly.

Akriti got all excited but Anusha didn't reply.

"Papa is asking something Anusha", retorted Seema.

"It is difficult to take a leave from the office. There is a lot of work pending."

"You were working even on Christmas. Won't they give a few days off", asked Seema.

"I don't want to go anywhere, Ma!"

"How long will you keep mourning? It has been six months since that accident. Why can't you let it go?"

Akriti quietened Seema down who had become a bit hysterical. Anusha picked up her bag and left for the office without saying anything or finishing her breakfast. She had gotten frustrated with everyone trying to fix her.

CHAPTER 4

Anusha was the Regional Manager at Corporate Bank. She was always a hard-working student with an above-average mind which got her one of the best placements in college. She had been working for three years now and after Karan's death, she occupied herself in her job completely. But off late something was not right. She had not been feeling herself for a long time. Her work had started suffering and her colleagues were almost annoyed with her lingering grief. No one around her could understand her deteriorating mental health except Shruti. She was three years elder than Anusha and was married to a loving husband and had an adorable daughter. When she got pregnant, her husband took care of her entirely and after the delivery, he took paternity leave to take care of their daughter. They were a good couple and seeing Shruti, Anusha was always reminded of Karan and how her life could also have been similar, blissful and fulfilling. Shruti constantly made efforts to cheer Anusha up when the rest of the people in the office had given up on her. Shruti had lost her mother at the age of fifteen and she knew how the grief crawls slowly inside never allowing the person to recover fully. Shruti's husband helped her heal. His love made her forget the pain and suffering of her loss. That Anusha also deserved love in her life again stopped Shruti to interfere after a certain point.

Anusha was working in her cabin when Shruti came and pat her back.

"I, Niharika and Vani are planning to go to "Toit" tonight. Will you come along?"

"Not today, I am drained out from the training and travel," Anusha replied disinterestedly.

"Come on Anusha. It is the last weekend of the year. You have to come."

Shruti made an endearing face to persuade Anusha and she finally agreed.

The pub was crowded. It seemed like the new year had already arrived. The spirits of people were high, bidding a fair farewell to the present year. But Anusha was feeling quite the opposite. Music was pricking her skin like a thousand needles. Shruti came with a tray of tequila shots which all four of them guzzled down after raising a toast. It left a bad after-taste in Anusha's mouth. She was still recuperating from that when Shruti dragged Anusha to the tiny dancing space on the floor. It was Anusha's favourite song from the Beatles. "Love, Love me do" filled the air with its syrupy lyrics. Everyone was grooving except Anusha. The music was hitting her head badly as the song reminded her of Karan. Beatles were not only her favourite but Karan's favourite too. That was the first song which he had sent to Anusha when they started dating. Anusha felt dizzy and everything around her became hazy. No longer able to take it, she hurried out of the pub, gasping for breath. The wisp of wind allayed her discomfort. The memories of cheerful times with Karan flashed before her eyes and she felt light and breezy.

When Anusha returned home, Akriti was still up working on her case.

"You are home already! What about the party?"

Anusha went back into her room not replying to Akriti. Akriti followed her.

"What happened Sha?"

"Will you come and sleep here today?"

Akriti looked at Anusha. She was looking ruffled and out of space. Akriti hugged Anusha tightly.

"Shall I say something, Sha?" "You should go and consult a psychiatrist again."

"I don't need one. I am already taking the medicine every day. He said it will help."

"He also said you have to visit again. You need counselling, someone who can listen to you and your fears."

"You are here with me; I don't need a counsellor. I can talk to you anytime I want. Can't I?"

"You can Sha!" "But the trauma is making you feeble. I can't see you in pain like this."

"Okay, I will go tomorrow," Anusha replied to a distraught Akriti.

Akriti pulled the blanket and cuddled Anusha. They both slept off like kids, peacefully.

Anusha reached outside the psychiatrist clinic and parked her car. She kept her head on the headrest and took a moment before going inside. She grabbed the steering wheel tight. Then instead of going in she started the car, took a U-turn and drove away from there.

She reached home to find everyone settled down for dinner.

“Here she comes, we were talking about you,” said Seema.

“Anything special?” asked Anusha desultorily.

“We were talking about your marriage. Sharma uncle had called. He had asked for your hand for his son." "He is the Senior Manager in a private company". "We thought you should meet him once,” Pradip said all that in one go without giving any space for Anusha to respond.

"What are you talking about, Papa?" "You know I am still not over Karan." "How can I marry someone else."

“Sha doesn’t need to get married, she needs a psychiatrist. She gets panic attacks.”

“Psychiatrist! She is not going crazy to go to a psychiatrist. She just needs a change of environment. That is why we were planning to go to Ooty. You can meet Sharma Uncle's son after we come back". "A change of scenery will do you good," Seema explained. She refused to admit that her daughter needed a psychiatrist as if it was a trivial thing and nothing to get worried about.

Anusha who was listening to all this flipped out.

"Will you people stop it? I don't need anything, no marriage, no psychiatrist." "Please leave me alone." She hurried into her room and banged the door. She was furious.

Akriti came in feeling guilty for pushing Anusha to see a therapist and for the discussion that ensued. She was also angry at her parents for not understanding Anusha enough and not giving her space.

"Sha! Do you remember you used to write an anonymous blog in college? It was so popular. Karan also loved it. Why don't you write a blog again, where you can express your feelings, kind of a catharsis?"

"Please do think about it." "And I know Ma-Papa were wrong today." "Try to not take it to your heart. They don't know how to help you."

Akriti left the room and Anusha broke down bitterly curling into herself.

CHAPTER 5

The Day I Realised I Am Alive

"Sometimes we feel that person who has died has left us. But that is not true. Death doesn't take the person away. It brings him closer. Closer in memories, in heart, mind and in the soul."

Anusha was reading the end of her Instagram post on her phone. It had gathered some likes. Anusha was scrolling through the comments of the people who had also lost a loved one at some point in their lives. She felt a shared connection with them and felt a little relieved of the burden of her feelings.

Her boss called her to his cabin. Anusha knew what it was about. She had yet not completed the loan file of "Shukla and Brothers." She knocked on the cabin and saw Mr Tripathi serious and perplexed. Mr Tripathi was a congenial man and he was fond of Anusha. She was a sincere employee and he was upset at her incompetence and the frequent delays.

"You need to get your act straight, Anusha." "This is for the second time I am calling you for the same thing. Please make sure the file reaches me tomorrow."

Anusha stepped out of the cabin and felt restless. The sense of relief which she was feeling a while ago had gone. It had turned into something sour and unpleasant. Shruti who had been watching Anusha since she had entered Mr Tripathi's cabin walked up to her and asked her to accompany her to the terrace for a cup of coffee. Vani and Niharika were already there smoking their cigarettes. Anusha used to be close friends with them at one point in time. They used to take coffee breaks together and laugh and gossip. But now, like many others, they were insensitive towards what she was going through and could not understand her predicament.

Anusha joined them nonchalantly.

“Snap out of it, Anusha. Tripathi called me yesterday. He has a habit of showing his authority to his employees. Don’t be sensitive. It is not that big a deal. Just get over it,” remarked Niharika.

Anusha started feeling uncomfortable. She excused herself and went back to her cabin.

“You are unbelievable, Niharika!” Shruti elbowed Niharika and rebuked her.

“I was just talking. She has to pull herself up someday or the other. Everyone has their struggles. No one said life would be easy. We are doing the best we can.”

Shruti felt bad about Anusha but didn’t know what to do.

Anusha was in her cabin, oblivious to the fact that her face had become moist with tears. Just then her phone rang. Anusha regained consciousness and wiped her tears hastily. It was her cousin Megha who had called to invite Anusha to Pune. She was about to deliver her first baby and she wanted Anusha to be there for the delivery. Megha was excited and Anusha for a minute, forgot about her grief and became joyous with Megha.

CHAPTER 6

Anusha lifted Megha's daughter in her arms and felt soothed, a feeling which had been elusive to her for a long time. The baby yawned and it made Anusha laugh.

"Welcome to the world, Sleepy eyes!"

Vineet, Megha's husband, and Megha were pleased to see Anusha.

Megha and Anusha shared an affectionate bond. Since childhood, they were like-minded. They both chose finance as their major, loved Murakami and had the same passion for music. They would love to listen to Beethoven and the Beatles for hours. After doing her major Megha opted to work for an NGO which facilitated micro-finance for rural women. Vineet also used to work in the same NGO and theirs was a love marriage. Though a brilliant person, Megha was never over-ambitious and always wanted a simple life. Anusha was proud of Megha and the kind of life she had made for herself. Megha was the first person to whom Anusha had told about Karan. It was important for Anusha that Megha liked Karan before she made him meet her family and Megha found Karan to be perfect for Anusha.

The nurse came in and handed over a list of vitamins to Vineet. Anusha offered to buy the medicines, carefully put the baby in Megha's lap and headed towards the pharma.

Anusha walked through the hallways which were painted in grim blue and greyish white colour. The dispensary was outside the main building near the entry gate along with the canteen. A car which was parked on the porch in front of the dispensary moved away from her sight and Anusha saw Aman standing there looking a little dishevelled. Anusha staggered to her feet. His beard had grown and when she greeted him he didn't recognise her. The mention of Murakami brought him out of his weariness. He became apologetic for not remembering Anusha.

"Sorry, I am a little preoccupied. It is such a pleasant surprise to meet you here."

"Do you remember, I told you my cousin stays in Pune? She just delivered a baby girl," Anusha mentioned excitingly. "What about you, how come you are in a hospital? I hope everything is alright."

"Actually, not. My mother is not well, cancer, fourth stage."

It came as a shudder to Anusha. She became silent while trying to find words to say to Aman.

The pharmacist kept Aman's medicines at the counter.

"Can I come and visit her?"

Aman nodded and told Anusha the room number.

Anusha knocked on the door and entered the room. The room looked well inhabited as if they were in there for several days. Aman was resting on the sofa. He got up when he heard the knock. Anusha walked in and saw Aman's mother sound asleep. She sat there for some time, wordlessly looking at Aman's mother. Then she saw Aman's face. It looked pallid.

"You should eat something," said Anusha to bring Aman out of the crushing situation and that bleak room.

She brought a coffee for both of them and a sandwich for Aman from the canteen counter.

"I know you like sandwiches."

Aman smiled out of gratitude.

"Thanks. I never thought we will meet again." "How are you otherwise?" Aman asked, putting in a lot of effort to pull those words out of him. He had not talked to anyone in the past few weeks.

"Still coping. But today is a good day for me. So, won't bother about the past."

"Don't you have anyone else with you here, your dad?"

"My father passed away when I was 16. Heart attack."

"I am sorry, I should not have asked."

"I miss him but I no longer rue over the fact that he has left us. Losing my mother scares me. The fear that I will be alone frightens me. And seeing her in pain hurts a lot."

A tear seeped down the corner of his eye and Aman removed his spectacles to clean them and dabbed it furtively.

Anusha hesitatingly clutched at his hand. The whole canteen became non-existent to her. She could only see Aman and felt one with his pain.

Part 2

CHAPTER 7

The house looked unfamiliar and strange and Aman felt as if he had entered an empty, alien space. He looked around and saw the paint on the walls chipping. Rains had added to the wear and tear leaving the house damp, glum and insipid. The plants have died with no one to take care of them in the past month. A sudden dryness in his throat stung Aman and he went to the refrigerator, picked up a bottle of water and drank desperately. He heard a flutter and saw a pigeon which had just flown into his mother's room, from the window he had forgotten to close. A ray of light was falling on his mother's bed and the pigeon was walking on the floor and flapping and grunting as if it had lost its way. Aman tried to shoo it away but it kept jumping and eluding him. He finally gave up and sat on his mother's bed as lost as the pigeon, not knowing what to do and where to go from there. He curled on the bed holding his mother's blanket and slept away like a child. His mother had passed away.

When he woke up it was already 7.30 in the evening. The sun had set and it was dark. Aman kept lying on the bed in the darkness with his eyes wide open. He neither had the strength nor the courage to get up. The sound of the wall clock ticking was the only sound to be heard. The silence was disturbed by the piercing sound of the thunder which shook Aman out of his distressing state. He felt a pang of hunger. He had not eaten anything since morning. He eventually got up, switched on the lights and walked down the living room to the open kitchen. The sofa, the dining table, the coffee table, the chairs and the stools, all of them looked overbearing. Aman felt scared and shut his eyes. It had started raining now and the clouds were rumbling.

Mustering all the courage, he opened his eyes and decided to make some tea and bread for himself. He took out the pan, poured a cup of water, added some tea leaves, milk powder and sugar and left it for boiling. He then opened the refrigerator and took out some bread and butter. He toasted the bread and spread the butter and ate it slowly while sipping his tea. It was so silent that he could hear himself chewing. He sat there on the dining table alone, and when a tear dropped into his mug, he realised he had been crying all this while.

CHAPTER 8

Yukta rang the bell the tenth time and when Aman opened the door, she barged in furiously, not out of anger but out of concern. The house was in shambles. She turned to see Aman's messed up face, his unkempt hair, long overgrown beard and tattered clothes.

"What have you done to yourself and why are you not picking up my calls? I knew I would find you at home."

Aman kept silent. Yukta held his hand and took him to the bathroom.

"Go have a shower first, then we will talk." She grabbed a towel and thrust it into Aman's hands. She then went to the cupboard to take out some fresh clothes. Aman complied silently.

She made some tea and took out biscuits from the cabinet in the kitchen. Aman came out and sat beside her at the dining table. If not better, he was surely looking clean now. They both sipped the tea silently.

"Will you say something? I know we are no longer together, but we are still friends."

Aman kept silent. Yukta clasped his hands and tears rolled down Aman's face. Yukta also became vulnerable but she composed herself.

"Aunty is gone Aman, but you are still alive. You can't hurt yourself like this. You have to live for yourself. I know it's hard but you have to try."

Aman broke down and started crying bitterly holding Yukta's hands.

Yukta had left Aman because of his distant behaviour. She could not feel his presence. He was always somewhere else, consumed by his problems and not even discussing them with her. She tried so much to understand him, to support him but she always felt like an added burden. Whenever they met Aman kept on posing to be happy when in reality, he was not.

"Why did you leave me, Yukta?"

"You were lost and you left me with no choice."

"Will you forgive me?"

Yukta smiled and held Aman in her embrace.

"I don't have any hard feelings, Aman."

Aman clenched her hand tightly like an innocent baby.

CHAPTER 9

A cold, arid breeze was ruffling Aman's hair while he was running on the muddy path with his headphones on. He came near the old Banyan tree, stopped there and bowed down gripping his knees. He was sweating profusely from all the running. He looked up into the sun, which was bearing him down with intimidating rays.

It had become his daily routine and the only few hours of the day where he vented out all his frustration and angst. The angst of being left alone in this world. He thought he was prepared for it. But nothing could prepare one for the devastating loneliness after one's parents were gone. The Banyan tree gave Aman a sense of security and a much-needed refuge. He sat underneath its cool shade every day and felt relaxed and peaceful for some time.

He came back home and went straight for the shower. The shower was pouring heavily on him and Aman stood below it as if washing away all the pain and suffering. He stepped out wiping himself and picked up his mobile to check his daily appointments but instead, stared blankly at the screen. He kept scrolling through his Instagram and noticed a suggested post. Its heading read, "The day I realized I am alive." He clicked on the link and went on to read one of the posts:

"Sometimes the things that make you are the ones that break you,

And collecting the broken parts you have to keep moving,

For it is only you in the beginning and you in the end,

And in between are the differences you make, for good."

The post held Aman's attention. He checked the name of the writer.

It was a personal blog written under the name "Anonymous". He clicked on the follow button on the Instagram account, kept his phone on the side and went to the kitchen to prepare some breakfast.

CHAPTER 10

It was twilight. The stars were not yet out but the moon was peeping from Aman's bedroom window. Aman took his antidepressant medicine and put on some classical music to assuage his grief. The day had gone by without doing anything. He was eating his three meals a day but had still not got the energy to go to his clinic and attend to his patients. Aman was a successful psychiatrist and ran his clinic with the name "Beautiful Minds". Being a psychiatrist he knew the five stages of grief – denial, anger, bargaining, depression and acceptance. He was not in denial and was no longer angry at his situation. But he was unhappy and lonely. For the past few years when his mother was unwell, he didn't get the time to mull over his situation. Taking care of his mother and listening to his patients had kept him occupied. Now suddenly there was a void. A void he didn't know how to fill. The medicines and his run in the morning were helping him to cope with the unbearable sadness and grief. But the void existed making him fragile every day.

Aman was deep in the music when a notification popped on his mobile. "Anonymous" had posted something new. Aman read it eagerly.

"O' Wind will you come again,

the falling droplets can you heal,

the flying birds and your drifting feathers,

Will you go to my loved ones as you come to me!"

The words moved within him. He started scrolling and read a few other posts.

"Lying in your arms fast asleep,

my eyes closed and your eyes on me,

I felt maybe, what angels would have felt,

when they had their first wings!"

Aman went further and read another post.

"Yesterday night, raindrops fell on my face, like pearls of solitude. The wind was crashing through my body and I could see the whole city melting. Melting like my face in the rain. And I thought, "Are life and death part of the same coin? Does grief need to be understood or be accepted as a part of life?"

Aman read that post and paused. He felt as if the posts were speaking to him. He gazed at the shining moon and after a while fell into a deep, peaceful slumber.

CHAPTER 11

The next day when Aman went for his daily run and sat in the shadow of the Banyan tree, he heard the birds chirping for the first time. Amongst the sparrows, he noticed a lone solitary bird with a yellow torso and green beak, exactly the one described in the blog post.

"Oh! The bird, with the yellow torso and green beak

the one which perched on my wire

having the courage of the whole world

Tiny and yet so full

you came as a whisper of love

and took me with you"

He was astonished at the coincidence and it changed something within him. He no longer felt like a stranger in his own body. The crippling loneliness vanished for some time.

That day Aman came back from his run smiling, content and in control of his emotions.

He cleaned the house and organized his room. He watered the plants, checked his appointments and decided to go to the clinic for the first time after months.

Aman's clinic was half an hour away from his house at Apte

Road. The clinic was situated amidst a green plush locality with trees all around. Aman had realised long ago that he had a special relationship with trees. During his childhood when a tree at his colony was cut down, as it was in the middle of the road and was disrupting the traffic, he cried for days and didn't take his food. It was only after his parents gifted him a jade plant that he came back to normality.

The clinic was austere with pastel-coloured walls. There was a space for Aman's secretary, Neha, at the entrance with a calendar of mountains and forests and rivers and waterfalls hanging above her table. Aman's desk had a vase that Neha filled every day with flowers when he had appointments. For that day, too, she had brought him orchids which she carefully placed in the vase. The purple flowers filled the otherwise bare room with a colour of sanguinity.

At the clinic, he listened to his patients intently. He was spacing out often in the middle of his sessions but managed to keep them afloat.

Neha was pleased to have Aman back. She had been with Aman for five years. She was married with two kids and considered Aman like a younger brother. She offered to take him out for lunch to which Aman said yes. He was not running away from people anymore. In the absence of a real family, he realised he already had one which he had been ignoring, his work, his patients and his friends. This reminded him to call and meet them.

CHAPTER 12

It was Saturday night and the pub was full of people. Aman was sitting at the bar with Rajat and Himanshu, drinking beer. Rajat and Himanshu were Aman's school friends. They had been together for years. Rajat was tall, lean and had a sincere look on his face. He was the most dependable of them. Himanshu had a charming and chubby face which made him look affable. Aman and Himanshu were known in school for their pranks. But when Aman's father passed away he became a bit solemn. Himanshu and Rajat were the only ones who stood by his side and comforted him. They had been together for so long that they understood each other without saying much. That's why when Aman avoided them they waited for him to come out of the mourning and sadness. But they still showed their displeasure at him for not picking up their calls.

"You have put at stake eighteen years of friendship just like that." "We got tired of calling you," said an upset Himanshu.

"We also came and rang the bell of your house but no one answered. We thought you must have gone to the clinic and didn't want to disturb you there." Rajat said with apprehension.

"I was badly shaken and didn't feel like meeting anyone," Aman said apologetically.

"Yukta was also worried. I guess she met you once?" asked Rajat.

“Yeah, she came home. We talked for a while but then I didn’t want to call and bother her. She has moved on with Nishant and I didn’t want to interfere.” Aman said looking down at his pint of beer.

Himanshu kept his arm on Aman’s shoulder lovingly, “We understand that you didn’t call Yukta but you should have replied or called us back. We were so worried.”

Aman became emotional and apologised to them.

The dance floor was full and all three of them were looking at the people blankly.

“Let’s go to Goa,” Himanshu exclaimed. “We need a break.” “There is a music festival happening there next month and our favourite singer is playing.”

“You mean Opeth!” remarked Aman.

“I am in. I haven’t been on vacation for the last two years. The job is taking a toll on me.” Rajat became all excited.

“It’s decided then. Next week, South Goa, I will book the tickets.” Himanshu said, raising his pint of beer for a toast.

Aman and Rajat clinked it with their bottles enthusiastically.

Aman took his sip and felt a baggage lifting from his shoulder. He had a good feeling about the trip. The music was flowing and he started grooving unknowingly. Rajat and Himanshu laughed at seeing him and joined him on the dance floor.

PART 3

CHAPTER 13

The waves were rising and ebbing and crashing on the golden sands of the Mobor beach in Goa like glistening marbles made of water being strewn on the floor. Opeth was playing his popular numbers. A songwriter and singer, Opeth had grown on the music scene in the past few years. It was Aman, who had introduced Rajat and Himanshu to his songs. His songs were transcendental and listening to them in the backdrop of the tranquil beach gave Aman some peace. All three of them were having their beers when Aman spotted a familiar face in the crowd. It was Anusha.

She was sitting alone on the sand enjoying the music and having her martini. Aman, surprised at the coincidence, excused himself from his friends and went up to her. Anusha was rapt in the music when Aman tapped on her shoulder and sat beside her. Anusha though startled, was elated to see him and embraced him.

"You have come alone?"

"I needed a break from everything."

"I hope I am not disturbing you. If you want I will leave."

"Oh no! You can stay."

Aman smiled and gushed.

They kept listening to Opeth for the rest of the evening quietly without saying anything. After a while, the songs became their words. Anusha leaned her head upon Aman's shoulders and the music and the sound of the waves filled the air around, enveloping them.

CHAPTER 14

Rajat and Himanshu retired to their rooms. Anusha and Aman decided to take a stroll on the beach. They started walking amidst the frothy milky waves which were collapsing between their bare toes like soap bubbles.

"Can I ask you something?" Aman said breaking the silence between them.

Anusha nodded in affirmation.

"What triggered you that day at the airport?"

Anusha paused for a moment and Aman waited for her to reply.

"The newlywed couple reminded me of my fiancé Karan. He died in a car accident just before our marriage. I survived and I still hold myself responsible for that mishap. If he would not have been distracted by me he would be still alive."

"You can't blame yourself. It was an unfortunate accident."

"I guess it was my destiny."

"You believe in it?"

"There are so many things which happen beyond our control. I guess that is destiny."

"But what we make out of them, the choices we make,

determine who we are and how we shape our lives."

"Are you able to shape yours?"

Aman knew Anusha had become a little uncomfortable with his questions but he didn't budge from the truth and the reality. Unlike Anusha, he had accepted his fate and had made peace with it.

"After my mother passed away. I was heartbroken. But then I decided to live each moment with joy and be grateful for what I have rather than what I lost."

"Everyone around me is forcing me to move on but how much ever I try, I can't forget Karan."

"You can't forget him just like I can't forget my parents."

Anusha felt relieved as if for the first time someone could understand what she had been going through.

"Do you feel alone sometimes?" She asked of Aman.

"Yes, I do. A lot."

"So do I."

A sky lantern hovered above them and for a while they both forgot their grief and followed its trail till it got lost in the starlit sky. A stream of sky lanterns followed the first one and the whole sky was lit up with the flying lights. Anusha held Aman's hand and Aman for the first time looked at Anusha's face closely, radiating in the light emanating from the lanterns. Her brown hair, her melancholic eyes which were now twinkling and reflecting the sky lanterns, her high cheekbones and her dewy rose-pink lips. He felt a seizing urge to kiss her but he held himself back.

CHAPTER 15

Aman walked with Anusha to her cottage. They said goodbye to each other unwillingly. Anusha shut the door of her room but kept standing by it, hoping for Aman to return. Aman turned and began to walk towards his room when he decided to go back and rang Anusha's room's bell. She opened it immediately and Aman held her in his arms and kissed her. Anusha, who was waiting for that kiss, surrendered herself in Aman's arms.

He brushed his hands in her wavy hair and showered her face with his kisses. He caressed her forehead, her eyes and her nose and kissed her lips again passionately. Anusha's lips quivered and Aman stopped. He looked at Anusha and saw a tear leaving a trail till her ears. He held Anusha tightly and she trembled and started sobbing. Her grief had engulfed her again. Aman pulled the sheets and wrapped her in them, cuddling her and not letting her go. Anusha wept for some time and slept away in Aman's arms with her face pressed to his chest. For the rest half of the night, Aman kept stroking Anusha's forehead.

It was morning and the lit-up Church bells, seen from the window of the cottage, sang the alluring hymn waking up Aman. He sat up and looked around. The pebbled walls, the copper water jug lying on the bedside table, the reclaimed wood furniture and the tapestry hung up on the wall adjacent to the window, everything seemed illuminated like Anusha's face sleeping beside him. She was no longer in his arms and Aman felt incomplete for the first time in all these years. He wanted to give her a morning kiss, make breakfast for her and see her relishing it, but he just sat there looking at her.

Anusha stirred and Aman distracted himself to get water. She pulled herself out from the sheets and saw Aman quietly sipping water and pretending to give her space. She felt the warmth of his embrace lingering on her. She looked towards him and Aman felt Anusha's eyes on himself. A sudden vulnerability overcame him. He knew if he would turn he would no longer be able to hide the truth, which they both knew by now, that he had fallen in love with her.

"You want to catch on some breakfast?" Aman asked, swiftly getting up from bed to shake off the awkwardness.

Anusha's concerned face turned into a smile and she nodded.

They sat together in a big hall where there were a series of tables. It was the common dining room of the hotel. A vase full of roses was there on each table. Anusha's face lit up with a smile looking at the roses. She looked at Aman who had already seen them and was blushing a little. They ordered pancakes with chocolate spread and some coffee to go along with them. They ate their breakfast quietly sharing glances in between. They both kept silent but looked extremely happy. The chatter in the dining room filled the space between them.

CHAPTER 16

Aman was sitting in the reception. The thought of leaving Anusha was making him restless. He was incessantly shaking his feet waiting eagerly for Anusha when he saw her strolling towards him with her suitcase. She was wearing a pink kurta and pants and was looking delicate but confident. Aman's heart skipped a beat but he collected himself. Anusha came near him to say the final goodbyes and before she could say anything Aman spoke.

"When can I see you again?"

"Will you give me your number?"

"5432789"

Anusha saved it and Aman wanted her to share her number and give him a call but she didn't. Instead, she hugged Aman, said "Thank you" and left. Aman stood there frozen, looking at her leaving while fidgeting with his phone. His friends called him. He went back to his friends hiding his sadness. They sat in a cab and left for Pune.

Anusha reached home and could not forget Aman. Karan was slowly becoming a past but he had left an emptiness. She thought of calling Aman a lot of times but realised that she only felt the urge when she was feeling alone. She wanted to make a fresh start rather than fill up the black hole which had crept inside her.

Akriti saw a change in Anusha. She was less vulnerable and had started to do those things again which she used to enjoy but had stopped pursuing. She looked motivated and so was Aman.

Aman was still waiting for Anusha's call. He knew Anusha needed time. And things around him kept on making him believe the connection they had made. There was an air of positivity around him and he was feeling good within. The longing had made him calmer instead of angry or bitter.

PART 4

CHAPTER 17

"I lost my fiancé before my marriage. It had been a year, and I could not forget him. I started writing these posts to heal myself whenever I got overwhelmed with my feelings. But grief sometimes takes over you when you least expect it. Recently I met a stranger who restored my faith in life. It is because of him that I could share my aching heart today. He made me feel that the world can be as positive as you believe and as negative as you think."

Sitting at his workstation, Aman read the post again and again. He could not believe the post he was reading. The doorbell rang. It was a speed post. He opened the envelope and it was an invitation from the "Mental Health" foundation. Aman read the letter and found that he had been invited as a guest speaker in a seminar on Post Traumatic Stress Disorder (PTSD) in Coorg.

Something struck in him. He hurriedly came back to his room and wrote them a mail to call the "Anonymous" writer he had been following.

For the next week, Aman carried on with his regular life - going on his morning run, preparing breakfast for himself and washing the dishes, receiving his patients, going out for a stroll sometimes in the evening to take fresh air and meeting his friends on weekends. Meanwhile, he kept waiting for the reply from the foundation. The seminar was next month and something inside him kept telling him that the anonymous writer was Anusha.

It was the usual day of the pre-monsoon. The sun was shining leaving orange hues in the sky. Aman was having lunch with Neha when his phone chimed. The foundation had replied and accepted his suggestion to invite the anonymous writer. Aman yelled a silent "Yes," and Neha was startled to see him this excited. Aman blushed and tried to brush off his excitement but Neha understood. She had been noticing a change in Aman since he had come back from Goa. Neha understood that Aman was in love. She was happy for Aman.

CHAPTER 18

It was raining continuously in Coorg. Aman got out of the cab and rushed inside the hotel. The bellboy took his luggage and showed him his room. Aman freshened up, prepared some coffee in the electric kettle and settled down on the covered terrace of the room.

The hotel had a serene stream flowing by its side and was surrounded by hills and coffee plantations. The whole place was soaked in rain and had turned lush green like Aman's heart. Aman waited eagerly for the seminar while looking at the turquoise-blue water of the stream.

The seminar hall was not that big with some twenty delegates who were invited from India and abroad. The speakers had expertise in psychiatry, research, journalism, writing, mental health activism and neurosurgery. Aman was talking to one of his colleagues when he saw Anusha walking in, trying to figure everything out. She looked a little bewildered as the whole idea of being the guest speaker at a mental health seminar was unfamiliar to her and she was surprised at the invitation which had reached her. She managed to find a comfortable seat in a private corner of the hall.

Aman saw her sitting relaxed in her seat looking around curiously. He excused himself from the conversation and sat in the front row seats to avoid being spotted by Anusha.

His whole life rolled over his eyes and Aman accepted that destiny had given him another chance to start a family and have a new beginning.

The host greeted them all and invited speakers to share their thoughts. She called Anusha on stage. Though nervous, she took the mic decisively. She spoke about her grief and how she overcame it and lightened herself by writing her feelings in her posts. She shared how sometimes people close to you could not understand your feelings and pain, and strangers could provide relief and understanding. She also shared how she was still afraid of going to a psychiatrist and taking her anxiety medicines, but she was trying to heal.

Her thoughts, experiences and journey got appreciated. Aman had a lump in his throat listening to Anusha. He wanted to hold her hand while she was speaking, but he decided to give her all the courage while sitting in the crowd. The host called on Aman, and Anusha, who had walked back to her seat and was about to sit, halted, hearing his name. She saw Aman walking up the stage, and her heart started beating so fast that she felt it would jump out of her chest. She heard Aman speaking about PTSD professionally. She heard him mentioning the importance of seeing a psychiatrist and seeking professional help and how medical science has helped several patients come out of trauma and be their normal selves again. She heard him highlighting the need to create awareness about mental health and remove the taboo attached to it. She heard him with her beating heart. She wanted to run away from there. She also wanted to yell at Aman for not telling her before that he was a psychiatrist. She wanted to bury her head and become invisible. She wanted to ignore the truth that Aman had been reading her posts all this while and had invited her to the seminar. She wanted to ask herself, "Was this meant to be!"

Anusha came back to her room and was flooded with thoughts and overwhelmed with feelings. Her mind and heart were at war. She was angry at Aman but at the same time could not forget what she felt about him; his sensitivity; his empathy; his care; and understanding.

She walked restlessly inside the room, and almost three hours had passed when Anusha looked at her watch. She pined and flumped on the bed. She closed her eyes, took deep breaths and realised that she could not bring herself to hate Aman. She packed her bags, checked out of the hotel and took a cab home.

CHAPTER 19

Aman came out of the seminar hall and looked around. He could not see Anusha anywhere. He asked the organiser about her and she told him that Anusha had already checked out from the hotel and had left. Aman's heart shattered and he sat down hopelessly. He knew he had lost her. He cursed himself for not telling Anusha before about his profession. He blamed himself for being fearful and insecure about losing her.

Aman came back to his room. He had to pack his stuff but he was not able to do that. His hands started trembling and for the first time since his mother's death, he did not want to go back home. He wanted to stay in Coorg and disappear in that room forever.

The intercom rang and the receptionist told him that the whole group had already checked out and they had booked his cab as well.

His phone beeped and it was a message from the airline that his flight had got delayed. His body shivered and a glimmer of hope ran along his limbs. Aman gathered his strength and packed his bags.

He reached Bangalore airport thinking about Anusha. The time spent with her was echoing in his veins.

CHAPTER 20

The two-hour road journey felt like an eternity to Anusha. Her mind was in thorough turmoil. The waterfalls and the coffee estates which she had cherished on her way to Coorg, she could no longer pay any attention to them. She wanted to reach home and talk to Akriti.

Akriti was not expecting Anusha so early.

"I hope everything is alright, Sha!"

"I don't know", Anusha replied confused.

Anusha then told Akriti about Aman; about their first meeting at the airport in Delhi and then in Pune and Goa. Akriti was baffled by the coincidences and Anusha was still perplexed about the fact that Aman was a psychiatrist. She told Akriti that she was upset at Aman for inviting her to the seminar.

Akriti listened to her patiently. She reminded Anusha of the change and optimism Aman had instilled in her life. Akriti also realised that it was not only Anusha who felt happier after meeting Aman, even Aman came out of his grief reading Anusha's posts.

"He also needs you, Sha, as much as you need him."

Anusha kept quiet for a while and then her heart accepted what her mind had been denying since then that she was also in love with Aman.

Aman was embroiled in his thoughts when his ringing phone woke him up from his ennui. It was an unknown number. Aman picked up the phone and recognised the voice.

"Where are you? I want to meet you."

“I am at the airport, sitting outside, in the cafeteria.”

“Don’t leave, I am coming.”

The airport was bustling with people just like the day they met for the first time. Anusha saw Aman waiting for her. She stopped and saw him from the distance. He was looking concerted yet his face was radiating composure. Anusha walked up to him unhurriedly.

Aman turned and stood up seeing her. She hugged him and Aman held her in his arms tightly. He then clasped her hand and asked,

“Where Shall we go?”

“Let’s go home.”

www.ingramcontent.com/pod-product-compliance
Ingram Content Group UK Ltd.
Pitfield, Milton Keynes, MK11 3LW, UK
UKHW042011190726
13854UKWH00005B/2247